The Silent Track Star

The Silent Track Star

by

Jerry B. Jenkins

MOODY PRESS
CHICAGO

ISBN: 0-8024-8239-2

2   3   4   5   6   Printing/LC/Year   90   89   88   87   86

Printed in the United States of America

To Don Jordan

Contents

1

Our Incredible Luck

The back screen door off our kitchen—the one my dad was forever reminding us to not let slam—was about to slam. I winced, but during the instant between when he breezed in and the smack, my best friend got in a half dozen words.

"You'll never believe who moved in!"

Smack!

"Dallas! Stop slamming that—"

Jimmy Calabresi, all dark and chunky, hair flying, round face beaming, bailed me out. "Sorry, Mr. O'Neil! It was me!"

My mother corrected him. "It was *I*."

Jimmy's brow knitted in puzzlement. He stared at me, then at her. "You don't have to lie for me, Mrs. O'Neil. It was *me*."

Mom shook her head.

I motioned for Jimmy to follow me to my room. "I'll bite. Who moved in, and where?"

"Toboggan Road, just off Baker Street. Travis Bourne."

I'm sure I looked doubtful. "Are you sure? *The* Travis Bourne?"

"One and the same."

"How do you know?"

"I was nosin' around down there when they were movin' in."

"Don't suppose you offered to help."

"They weren't movin' much. By the time I got there, they were almost finished."

"Jimmy, do you know for sure? I mean, this isn't going to be just another of your fits of wishful thinking is it?"

He held up his hand as if to swear his truthfulness. "I asked, him, Dal. I recognized him."

"That wouldn't be too hard with that white hair. Never saw a twelve-year-old with pure white hair before. I mean Brent's hair is awfully blond but not white like Travis's. But you talked to him? You didn't just figure him for Travis Bourne because he happened to have white hair?"

Jimmy looked hurt.

I apologized.

"Dallas, he didn't say much. but he did admit to bein' who he was. I tried to tell him all about the club, but his mother called him in. She didn't greet me or anything."

"She didn't? How about brothers and sisters?"

"I didn't see any."

"I thought sure he had one or two. Seems I saw them at last year's state meet."

Jimmy lay back on my bed and put his hands behind his head. He stared at the ceiling. "Me too. You gonna go welcome him to the neighborhood?"

"Guess I should."

" 'Course you should, Dal! We've got to get him in the club. You know he's got to be favored in the finals of the hundred, the two-twenty, the four-forty, and any relay he enters."

That was pleasant enough to think about. Any sports club, and especially any track team, would give just about anything to have a star like Travis Bourne. He was a legend in age-group track and field. I stood and moved toward the door.

Jimmy rolled to his side. "You going *now?*"

I nodded. "Shouldn't I?"

"I wish I could go with you, but I have to be home in a few minutes. I'll ride with you and show you where it is."

4

I was pedaling past the ramshackle house off Toboggan Road a couple of miles north of our place when Jimmy called after me. "This is it! Right here!"

I laughed. I thought he was kidding.

"I'm serious. This is the place."

I skidded to a stop, about fifty feet past the little house. I whispered. "This place isn't livable. Anyway, there aren't any lights on."

"I'm tellin' the truth, Dallas. About an hour ago, I saw Travis Bourne and his mom moving into this place."

There appeared to be a note taped to the mailbox by the road. Jimmy and I walked our bikes to it. "BOURNE." I cocked my head and shrugged. It was the first instant I realized that Jimmy was not putting me on.

"Gotta go. I'll call ya." He rode off.

The sun had slid past the tops of the trees in the west, but the sky was still light. The mosquitoes were out, and everything seemed to be in the shadows. As soon as Jimmy was out of earshot, I felt totally alone. No sound, no movement. Nothing.

Clearly, someone named Bourne had moved into that crummy little place that smelled musty even from fifty feet away. I had an urge to go see for myself, though it appeared no one was home. I hid my bike in the trees on the other side of the road and stepped lightly down the gravel driveway toward an ancient, one-car garage with doors that slid sideways and had little square windows at the tops. The garage was twenty feet deeper on the property than the house.

There was just enough light that I was able to make out the outline of an old car through the windows. Maybe someone *was* at home. But it was barely dusk. Would they be in bed with all the lights off already? I headed toward the house from the back, careful to stay on the grass and not make enough noise to scare anyone.

In the backyard was a small pile of boxes and some rickety furniture that looked as if it had not survived the move and which someone decided would be better off outside waiting for the garbage collectors.

This was a tiny house. I'd been in it exploring before. It went months, years sometimes, with no one's living there. If it was unlocked, it made a fun place to play, but for the last couple of years it had been off limits. A For Sale sign had been in the front for ages, and the realty company asked parents to help keep kids out of it.

The upstairs had two tiny bedrooms with no closets and no bathroom. Downstairs was a bathroom, the kitchen, a small bedroom with a closet, and the front room. That was it. From the back window I would see through the kitchen to the front room, and what I saw made me jump.

Someone was sitting on the couch in the living room, with her right side to the front window. It was obviously a woman. I could tell from the hair, but I couldn't tell how old or how well or anything. She would not likely have seen me come up the driveway, but if she turned her head even slightly to the left now she could have seen me peering through the kitchen window.

I stepped back and caught my breath. I knew the woman had to be Mrs. Bourne, but where was Mr. Bourne? And where was Travis? Maybe they were out together. But the car was in the garage. Maybe they had a truck too, like we did.

I moved around the north end of the house and up toward the front door, still out of sight in the growing darkness. The front door was open; the storm door, with screen, was shut. I was within a few feet of the front door when I heard low sobbing.

The woman was crying and sniffling, sitting there in the dark, alone. I felt so bad for her that I wanted to cry too. I wanted to just knock on the door and tell her everything would be all right, that there would be plenty of friends in the area, that moving was always tough, but that things would work out.

But I didn't know her. And I certainly didn't want to scare

6

her. How could I know what was making her cry? Maybe she was just tired. Suddenly I heard footsteps on the road. I squinted but couldn't see anyone. Luckily, whoever it was wouldn't be able to see me standing in the shadows at the front of the house either.

The steps were fast and were coming closer, but they were not the steps of someone in a hurry. They were steady, like a jogger's. In fact, as my eyes picked up the figure on the road, I knew it *was* a jogger.

He startled me by turning up the driveway. Now where was I supposed to go? I decided to go back around the same way I had come. It was a good thing, because Mrs. Bourne rose and turned on the front light outside, and if I had stayed where I was, I might as well have been on stage.

I was going to go around the back and up the driveway, but that's where the jogger was, so I just waited around the corner of the front of the house. The jogger turned left and slowed to a walk, then sat wearily on the front stoop and pulled down the hood of his sweatshirt.

Steam rose from his sweaty hair in the coolness of the evening. The hair was white. It was Travis Bourne. He sat with his elbows on his knees, his head bowed between his legs, his shoulders heaving as his breathing began to even out.

In a strange way, he looked the same way he would have if he had been crying. Could both mother and son be in such a mess that they were both crying? No. He wasn't. Just exhausted from a good workout.

His mother emerged from the living room, wiping her eyes and face with her apron. Her voice gave her away though. It was obvious she'd been crying. "Good run, son?"

"Yes, ma'am."

Both she and the boy had deep Southern accents.

"How far'd you go?"

" 'Bout three miles, I guess."

"Nice?"

He shrugged.

7

"Meet anyone?"

He shook his head.

"Did you run past that place where the other boy said the sports club captain lived?"

"Naw. Went the other way."

"Don't you wanna meet him, Travis?"

"I met him at the state meet last year."

"Run against him?"

"Think so."

"Beat him?" She smiled.

"Beat everybody." He didn't smile.

"You'd better cover your head again, son. You'll catch your death—"

But rather than pulling up his hood, he just stood and stretched and walked past her into the house.

I felt as if I were in a dream. Travis Bourne had moved into Baker Street Sports Club territory. If he joined us, there'd be no stopping us.

His mother sat out on the porch, her chin in her hand. She slapped at a mosquito, swore softly, and went into the house. The light went out, but now lights from two rooms glowed warmly in the night. I was able to slip away without being seen, and I waited on the other side of the road near my bike.

When I was sure Travis was out of the shower, I would head for the front door and knock. I had to meet this guy.

2

First "Chat"

I had always thought of myself as a sort of easy-to-talk-to kind of a guy. At least until that night.

Travis Bourne's mother answered the door, but she didn't say anything. No "Yes?" or "May I help you?" or anything. I was so sure she would at least greet me before I had to say anthing that I hadn't really thought of anything to start with.

I stood there not knowing where to begin. "Uh, hi. Is, um, Travis here?"

"Uh-huh." And she walked away. At least she didn't slam the door in my face. I didn't know if she was going to go get him, ignore me and leave me standing there, or get herself something to eat. I stood waiting.

Soon I heard snatches of their muffled conversation. Clearly, he didn't want to see anyone, and, just as clearly, she was making him go to the door. When he bounced into the living room, it was as if she had pushed him.

He was worse than she had been. He shyly approached the door, saying nothing. He had changed into shorts and a tee shirt and was wearing moccasins. He didn't introduce himself or make any attempt at greeting me. His body was silhouetted by the lights in the room, and I found myself staring at a dark form, unable to make out any of his features or look into his eyes or read whether he was smiling.

"Hi, uh, my name is Dallas O'Neil, and I'm captain of the Baker Street Sports Club. My friend Jimmy, Jimmy Calabresi, was by here earlier, and he said he told you all about our club, but then you would have already known about us because we ran against your suburban team in the state track finals last year."

I hesitated, but still I got no response. "That was some meet, huh? You took firsts in two events and seconds in two others, and only to that guy who'll be too old this year. Man, this'll be your year, right?"

He may have shrugged. I couldn't tell. It was eerie, standing there babbling into the darkness, but he wouldn't give me a thing. "We're the team who has the big twelve-year-old that everybody thinks is ineligible because he's so big. Jack Bastable, our shot put and javelin man. Six-four, almost two hundred pounds. But he's legal all right. Just big for twelve. Retarded, you know. Probably you knew that. Everybody knows that. He's a favorite."

I was fishing for any kind of a comment, but I wasn't even getting a nod or shrug, as far as I could tell. Still I kept on. "We have another big guy—Toby. He's nowhere near as big as Jack, of course, but he's our discus thrower. Throws about a hundred and twenty-five feet. Not bad for our age, huh?" No response.

"Jack never could figure out how to hold the discus right. He puts the shot over fifty feet and throws the javelin about a hundred and seventy-five. He'll do better this year. Toby wants to pole vault too, can you imagine? A big buy like that. But his best height is about eight feet, and I keep tellin' him that's only a couple of inches higher than the world record in the *high jump!*"

I fell silent for a moment to see what Travis might do. He was leaning and looked relaxed as if he didn't mind listening to someone talk about track and field, but he sure wasn't prepared to add anything. "So, you've moved into our area."

I said it as more of a statement than a question, and that's

12

the way he took it, because he didn't say anything. Maybe he thought it was so obvious that he had moved in that there was no need to say it in the first place. I thought about just telling him I'd see him around sometime, but my whole point was to get him in the club.

"Listen, we meet everyday after school in the shed between my house and our barn. We're there for about an hour, and we work out, jog, and all that. We'd love to have you join us. In fact, we'd give anything to have you in the club and on our team." I hadn't asked him if he would show up exactly, but I thought what I said deserved some sort of an answer. He must not have, because I didn't get one.

I felt stupid standing there talking to myself, but I was sort of stuck into it and had to keep going. "Jimmy—the one you met earlier today—he's a discus thrower too. We didn't know what else to do with him, with his size and everything. I don't mean that to put him down or anything. He's a real good athlete in a lot of other sports. And don't tell him I said anything about his track and field, because he's my best friend."

Why was I defending myself and what I had said to a guy who just stood there listening? Or maybe he was just standing there not listening. You couldn't have proved either way by me. "We have a good high jumper. He can go over five-six. Doesn't sound like much to high schoolers, but we twelve-year-olds know it's pretty good, don't we?"

He sniffed and rubbed his nose with his hand. I didn't know if he hadn't heard me or if that was his way of answering. I was so embarrassed—even though I thought *he* should be—that I just kept rattling on. "This high jumper is another good friend of mine, a redhead named Cory. He's real active and aggressive, something to watch."

"Our long jumper is a black kid we call Bugsy. He's also a quarter miler and runs on our mile relay team. A little blond kid named Brent is our other sprinter besides me. You ran against him in a relay leg last year. Remember?"

13

He shook his head. He actually shook his head! So he wasn't deaf or sleeping! "Bugsy runs the eight-eighty too, but he's not so good in that. He can do the quarter in less than seventy seconds, but his half mile is close to three minutes. Just runs out of gas. I don't blame him. We probably shouldn't even enter him in that event."

I started thinking of a plan. I didn't have any idea if it would work, but while I was talking, I was plotting. I had to find out what would get me next to this guy. So far, except for shaking his head about not remembering running a relay leg against Brent, he had been like a statue.

"Our miler is Ryan, another small kid. But he's got a lot of stamina. Maybe we should try him in the half, but he can't run both at his age. Rules, you know. Runs a five-thirty mile, which wins most dual meets."

It was time for my plan. "Well, I'd better get going. I was going to run around this long block—it's about a half mile—back to my bike across the street there, and then head home. I know you're the fastest twelve-year-old sprinter in the state, but I wouldn't ask you to run with me. I mean, I'm a sprinter too, but jogging long distances is really my specialty. I've discouraged a lot of sprinters with the way I jog. Kind of run them into the ground, you know? I can't get anyone, even in the club, to jog with me. Ryan sometimes. No one else dares. Well, gotta go. Hope to see you at our club soon."

I turned slowly to move away from his steps. I was in sneakers, long jeans, and a pullover shirt and was hardly dressed for jogging. My hope was that he would at least tell me that he had already been jogging and that he had done three hard miles so, "Maybe some other time." But I was too hopeful. He said nothing. I waved and began a slow trot.

From behind me I heard him call to his mother. "Be back in a few minutes!" The door slapped shut, and he cruised past me, looking over his shoulder as if to see if I was coming. I sped up to try to run with him, but it seemed he was loping pretty quickly for having to run a half mile, especially after his earlier workout.

I hadn't *really* wanted to run a hard half mile; I had only been trying to get him to say something. But now my honor was on the line, and, even though I wasn't dressed for it, I had to follow through. It was getting late, too. I would have to head straight home afterward.

I knew Travis would have to settle into a steady pace, and I kept watching for my chance to draw even with him. Every time we ran out of the light from a street lamp, I could hear him pick up the pace, as if trying to keep a lead on me in the darkness. We had gone maybe half the way around the long block when I realized that we were running at almost full speed. And Travis in moccasins!

I wondered what he would do if I caught him, but if we went much farther at that pace, I would have no strength left to try it. I decided to put all my effort into just catching and maybe passing him. If that took all the rest of my endurance, that would be all right. I wouldn't even mind stopping and walking and just obviously giving him the race.

But it wasn't supposed to be a race! We were just going to jog together, and I had concocted that craziness about discouraging other runners just to see if I could get any reaction out of him. It wasn't a lie exactly, because it was true that few people in the sports club could stay with me over a long distance, but I hadn't intended to challenge him to a race.

I shifted into high gear, my feet flying up behind me, arms pumping, head steady, chin down. I was going to catch him during a dark stretch between street lights if it killed me. I was suddenly sprinting at top speed, and the cool evening air rushed past my ears and combined with my pounding heart to block out all the other sounds.

I couldn't hear the insects or birds, and I didn't seem to be able to hear his footsteps either. I was flying, probably at a rate that would have covered a hundred yards in less than eleven seconds.

But as we came into the light again, I saw that he had accelerated. After having run the first quarter too fast—in my opinion—he was now holding off my fastest charge and was

15

actually putting distance between us.

I was embarrassed. Now I couldn't slow down and walk the way I could have if I'd passed him or even just caught him to show that I had something on the ball. If he heard me coming as fast as I could go and still blew me away, I'd be humiliated.

The sprint had taken everything out of me. My chest heaved, my throat was dry, my heart raced. But I had to keep going at a steady pace or lose a half mile run by a hundred yards. I strained to keep an eye on him, but he was pulling away.

3

Will He Come?

By the time we rounded the last corner and Travis Bourne's shacky house came into sight, my whole body was in pain. Travis was flying along lightly, hardly making a sound.

I wouldn't have been able to hear him anyway with the wind whistling past my ears, my breath coming in huge, long gasps, and my heart banging in my chest. He seemed to run without effort, and I was struggling just to keep going.

Rather than running up his driveway, Travis cut across his property and went straight for the front door. I figured he would sit on the steps and catch his breath and that that would give me a chance to finally stagger up.

Surely he would talk to me now, after we had shared the run. I wonder if he would have talked to me if I had beaten him. He would never have to worry about that. I glanced to my right to be sure my bike was still in the trees on the other side of the road, and then I angled toward Travis's door.

I stopped dead as I reached the front of his yard. The door had slammed. In fact, both of them had. The "race" was over, he was inside, and that was the end of that. I had to sit down. I had to get my head between my legs and let the blood return to my brain. I had to breathe deeply and replenish my oxygen supply. I felt like dropping onto the grass in his yard, but it was always easier when you could sit up on something. He wasn't going to talk to me, invite me in, offer me something to drink, tell me whether he would join the sports club or even visit a meeting, but still I had to use his front steps.

I dragged myself over to them and sat heavily, my legs sweating under my jeans. I spread my knees and rested my elbows on them, letting my head hang low, sucking for air. Suddenly I felt very sad, and I didn't know why. There was something strange going on in that house, in that family.

All I cared about was getting Travis Bourne into our sports club and onto our track team. It was disappointing to me to realize that I didn't care as much about Travis's personal problems as I did about what he could do for us.

The next day after school, Jack, Toby, Jimmy, Cory, Bugsy, Brent, Ryan, and I sat in our shed talking about how much stronger we would be with Travis on our team. Ryan was curious. "How would you use him, Dallas?"

"Any way he wanted to be used. He doesn't pretend to like or be good at the weight events, so I wouldn't expect him to put the shot or throw the javelin or discus. I mean, he's just my size, and even though he's strong, he wouldn't be able to do as well as Jack and Toby and Jimmy there. He's not a pole vaulter, and I don't think he high jumps—even though he'd probably be good at it."

Ryan was fidgeting. "So, that leaves the sprints, middle distance, and distance. He's a sprinter, isn't he?"

I nodded. "He also long jumps, you know. He's good."

"But what running events would he be in?"

"Well, obviously, the hundred and the two-twenty. Probably the four-forty."

"Not the distances then?"

"No, Ryan. Your event is safe. We might use him instead of you in the mile relay though."

"That doesn't bother me; I hate that mile relay. Everybody thinks the four-forty is an endurance event, but let's face it, anymore it's strictly a sprint, especially when you're running a leg of the mile relay."

Bugsy raised his hand. "Any idea if he can run the half?"

I couldn't hide a smile. " 'Fraid so. I jogged with him for about a half mile yesterday. At least *I* jogged. He smoked me. Ran me into the ground from the start."

"You?"

"Yup. Must've run well under three minutes."

Bugsy scowled. "So he might run the half."

"If we need him."

"And how will we know that?"

"By what our score is when we get to the half. But listen, you're our only other half miler, so whether he's in there or not, you will be."

"I'm not worried about running or not running. I'm worried about being number two man on my team in all three of my specialties—the quarter, the half, and the long jump. I suppose he'll replace me as anchor on the mile relay too."

"Even if he does, you'll still be in it. I already said that Ryan would probably be the one knocked out of that."

"Yeah, but I want to be the anchor man."

"You know we always run our fastest man last. Would you like to run first? I wouldn't mind running second or third."

Bugsy shrugged and shook his head, looking away. I reminded him—and everyone—that we always have to think of what's best for the whole team.

Each was worried about his own assignment, but there wasn't one of us who didn't want the fastest young runner in the state on the Baker Street Sports Club track team.

We were just breaking up when we saw him. He was jogging past our place on the other side of the road. He didn't look at us or even appear to know we were there, but he had to. Cory, the aggressive redhead, wanted some action.

"Get him over here, Dallas! Let's meet him."

I hadn't told the guys of the embarrassing experience I'd had the night before, and I certainly didn't want it to happen in front of them. "Oh, he's almost already past. We'll talk to him later."

21

"No! Now! Let's ask him to stop and talk to him and find out if he's gonna join us or not! That must be the reason he's running by!"

I still didn't want to, but what was I supposed to do? If I didn't approach him, they were all going to know something was up. I knew I'd have to do it loud and clear so that he would be too embarrassed to ignore me as he had the night before.

I ran directly into his path and stuck out my hand. He stopped but kept running in place, as if he wished I would get on with it so he could get back to his run. "Hey, Travis, how you doin', man?"

I hoped he would act as if he recognized me and admit that he was checking out the place where I told him we meet every-day. He just looked at me expectantly. "Listen, I want you to meet the guys in the sports club I was tellin' you about." I started to move toward them, but he didn't follow. So I quickly changed tactics. "C'mon over, guys! Meet Travis Bourne! You remember him, the fastest runner in the state!"

They crowded around, welcoming him to the neighbor-hood, shaking his hand, and all jabbering at once. "We could win the state this year with you on our team."

"We're good already, but you would put us over the top."

"We're the only thing goin' around here in track. You gon-na join us? Huh?"

Believe it or not, Travis Bourne finally said something. "We'll see."

With not even a nice-to-meet-you, he was off again, this time running faster, as if afraid we would light out after him.

Cory was the first to speak up. "Hey, Dallas, I thought you said he was as good as in the club. He sure didn't seem very friendly. I'll bet he doesn't even want to join us."

"We don't know that yet, Cory."

"Maybe not, but he sure doesn't look like he wants to get to know us."

"Or even speak to us."

"Yeah!"

"What's his problem?"

"Who cares? We have to get him in our club. He's your size, Dallas. Just sign him up and order him a uniform. Deliver it to his house and tell him when our next meet is."

"When is it?"

"A week from Saturday against Marymount."

"Good idea."

But when I got to Travis's house with his new uniform the next week, he wasn't there. I breathlessly told his mother that we had unanimously voted him into the club and onto the team and that we sure would like it if he would join us. "He knows where we meet; that's the same place we'll be working out tomorrow."

She slowly, almost hesitantly took the uniform. "Well, all right, son. I'll tell him." She had that tone of voice that speaks louder than the words themselves. What she was really telling me was that she couldn't guarantee that he would show up at the workout or the meet and that she wasn't sure how he would react to getting a uniform.

But I didn't want to hear that, so I plunged on. "Take a look at it, Mrs. Bourne. See, it's made of mostly nylon, so it's light and cool. The shorts are blue with red and white stripes on the sides, and the tee shirt is white with blue piping and a blue field with a red B on it. That stands for Baker Street, you know. We're the Baker Street Sports Club."

"I know."

The way she said that made me wish I hadn't said it. Of course she knew. She had a memory. I had introduced myself to her before. "Well, if you'll tell him, I'd appreciate it."

"I'll tell him."

"Bye."

She didn't say anything. She just shut the door, and I felt her eyes on my back as I hopped on my bike and pedaled away as fast as I could. That place made me nervous. Where was his father? Where were his sisters? Where was *he*?

We were in the middle of our workout the next day when the pessimistic ones in our club started predicting that Travis Bourne would never show up. "Not to a workout, certainly not to a meet, and you'll probably never see that uniform again." I was beginning to agree, even though I usually hope for the best until I'm proved wrong.

The guys were finishing up their individual workouts when I hollered that everyone should do an easy two miles around the long block in front of my house. We slowly jogged out onto the road and began a slow pace that left no one behind.

"Someone's coming!" Brent had said it. "Is it him?"

We all wheeled around, still running, and looked back down the road. I knew it was Travis, even from more than a quarter mile. The white hair was a dead giveaway. "All right! It's him! Now listen, don't say anything unless he does. He may just blow past us. If he does, let him go. Don't chase him, and whatever you do, don't hassle him. If he stays back there, just pretend you don't notice him."

He had shown up, maybe not to actually work out with us, but he had come by anyway. All the other guys' eyes were straight ahead. I stole a glance back. He was gaining on us, slow but sure.

4

Now What?

I began talking to the rest of the guys as we moved on down
Baker Street. As usual, there was no traffic, just the view of
farmland and the big interstate a half mile away.

"Don't speed up. Don't do anything differently. We're just
working out, we're not racing, especially not with Travis
Bourne. Easy. Easy."

But I could feel the guys picking up the pace. It wasn't as if
they were racing to stay ahead of him. It was really more that
they seemed to want to show off for him if and when he did
catch us. And it wouldn't be long.

If I hadn't already been shown up by him in my crazy half
mile idea several nights before, I might have been foolish
enough to try to impress Travis too. Now I just wanted to
make sure we didn't do anything that would make him not
want to join our club.

"If he catches up with us, just let him into the pack. Don't
bother him or talk to him unless he talks first."

That was hard advice to follow. The next time I looked
back, everyone else did too. He was there, just off Toby's
shoulder at the back. Toby was laboring, as he and Jimmy
usually did on these long jogs.

Travis wasn't content to stay there long. He began moving
up through the pack, past Jack and Cory, then even Ryan and

Brent. When he got near Bugsy, I noticed everyone running faster.

Bugsy couldn't resist a comment. "Welcome to the club."

I'm sure everyone—especially Bugsy—felt as awkward as I did when Travis didn't say anything. Of course, it didn't surprise me; I knew better than anyone that Travis wasn't much of a talker. But what had me worried was whether Travis was really joining our club or not. I mean, he hadn't returned the uniform, but that didn't mean he had joined either.

And here he was. But still saying nothing. Bugsy tried again. "We're going all the way around. It's about two miles. Gonna go with us the whole way?"

I turned in time to see Travis shrug.

Bugsy kept talking, though from his shortness of breath I could tell it was costing him. " 'Course you can just peel off at your place if you want. I mean, I don't know how long you've already been runnin' or anything. But if you're joinin' our club, I expect you'll be workin' out with us everyday, hm?"

Travis shrugged again and moved ahead of Bugsy. He moved up next to me but looked straight ahead.

"Hey, Travis. Good to see ya. How ya doin'?"

He nodded. At least he hadn't shrugged. "Have you run this two-mile course of ours before?"

He shook his head. "Don't much like talkin' while I'm workin' out."

Somehow, his saying even just that made me gabby. "Oh, I know what you mean. Neither do I. I mean, usually. But I was glad to see you joining us, that is, for this workout anyway. You decide when you're ready to join us for real, you know."

I looked over at him. No response. He was running fast, and I was struggling to keep up. This was ridiculous. I wasn't going to race him for two miles, not one of the best runners in the state. Long distance was not my strength, and it wasn't his either, but I guess he was in good enough shape and talented

28

enough in an all-around sort of way that it was no trouble for him.

I dropped back to let him go, but a couple of our more aggressive guys weren't about to let that happen. Toby and Cory came charging up, huffing and puffing and crudely trying to stay with Travis. Within a minute, he had buried them and was a hundred yards ahead of us.

I moved back up to the front of the pack and raised my hand, signaling everyone to stop and pull off to the side of the road. I put my hands on my knees and lowered my head, catching my breath. The others did the same. "Look, we're not going to win this guy over by competing with him or trying to talk to him. For some reason he doesn't want to talk, and so far he hasn't said he'll become part of the club, either. Let's just keep working out and leave him to his decision. I'm not going to push him anymore."

Toby kicked at the gravel. "Maybe we don't want him in the club if he doesn't want to make any new friends."

I didn't think it was that, and I said so. "He's just shy, I think. We don't even know why he moved here or where the rest of his family is. And he sure doesn't seem ready to talk about it."

Bugsy nodded. "Dallas is right. Let's just leave the guy alone and see if he decides to join us."

"But he just has to! We need him!"

I nodded. We sure did. But I didn't have a plan to push him toward us. We rolled back out onto the road, having stopped to talk for no more than a minute. Nearly a quarter of an hour later we struggled exhausted back into my yard and pulled on our sweat suits to retain the body heat we had built.

Not ten minutes later, Travis Bourne came running down the road. Was it possible? Could he have nearly lapped us, running four miles in just a little more time than it took us to run two? We were too stunned to even suggest it.

We were even more surprised when he slowed to a walk

29

and crossed the road to where we were sitting. We stared at him, but he ignored us. He took a position near a huge, old oak tree and just leaned against it, not breathing heavily, not sitting. It was as if he was waiting for us to begin some sort of a meeting.

I didn't want to disappoint him. "Now, guys, as you know, Saturday is the meet against Marymount. Remember that they are good in the sprints and the relays, have one good long jumper, and are weak in everything else. We should be able to beat them. I'll have all the final assignments Friday afternoon."

I turned to Travis. "If you're joining us, I'd like to officially welcome you and ask you how you'd like to be worked in Saturday."

With that, he was off running again, calling over his shoulder in his smooth Southern accent. "I'm still thinkin' about it."

We shook our heads. I had to comment on his ability. "It's becoming unbelievable. I knew he was good, but unless he found a ride or had a bike hidden somewhere, that guy just showed us what the competition is really like. Have you ever seen anything like it in your life?"

Cory spoke up. "I thought you weren't going to push him anymore."

"I'm not."

"Then why'd you badger him about joining?"

"I didn't! I was just saying—"

But I was met with such a barrage of agreement with Cory that I had to think back on what I'd said to the newcomer. Indeed, I had talked pretty specifically with him about joining us, and that went against everything I had pledged I would do.

I apologized to the rest of the guys. They accepted it, of course, but they still wanted a promise that I would back off of Travis Bourne and let him both run and think about joining our sports club at his own pace.

The next morning my mother found in our mailbox a note that was not in an envelope. In large, beginner's handwriting, Travis had printed: "I WOULD LIKE TO RUN FOR YOUR SPORTS CLUB SATURDAY. IF THERE IS ROOM, I'D LIKE TO RUN THE 100, THE 220, THE 440, AND THE MILE RELAY."

The note wasn't signed, and I didn't know if he needed a ride, one way, both ways, or not at all. If there is room!? He could run on any track team in the country. I wanted to see him in action.

On Friday afternoon I told the guys. They were excited. We sat in the shed in our sweatsuits, and I outlined who would be competing in what events. There weren't really any surprises. "Jack will put the shot and throw the javelin. Toby and Jimmy will throw the discus. Cory will high jump. Where is Cory, by the way?"

Brent knew. "He's late. He said to tell you he'll be here in a few minutes. Had to mow the yard, I think."

I nodded and continued. "Bugsy will long jump and run the quarter mile along with Travis."

Bugsy chuckled. "Along with him? Behind him, you mean!" Everyone laughed.

"Bugsy will also be in the mile relay. I'll run the hundred and the two-twenty with Brent and Travis, and the three of us will also be in the mile relay."

Ryan looked disappointed. "Then I'm out of the mile relay?"

I nodded. "You figured that, didn't you? I mean, you knew we'd have to go with Travis; we talked about it before."

He shrugged. "It's all right, I guess. I hope we can have time trials every week though so maybe I can win back my place on the relay team."

"You'll still be running the mile for us, you know."

"Yeah, but I want to get back on the relay team."

Toby snorted. "What're you gonna do, beat out Travis Bourne?"

31

Everyone laughed again, and Ryan waited until it was quiet. "Maybe I can beat out one of the other guys."

It was unlikely, and the slight shaking of several heads proved that most everyone agreed.

"What order for the mile relay, Dallas?"

I pulled a slip from my pocket. "I'll start, then Brent, then Bugsy, then Travis."

"Does he know that?"

"Travis? No. I haven't seen him since the other night. I'll let him know. Listen, do you guys all understand what he's gonna mean to this team?"

"Are you sure he's on this team, Dal?"

"What do you mean, Bugsy?"

"All his note said was that he would run Saturday. What if he quits after that?"

"Why would he quit?"

"Who knows? Why did he only write about Saturday when he could have said he had decided to join the Baker Street Sports Club?"

Toby shifted his weight. "Who cares? He'll join. Once he sees how good a team we are with him, he'll stick around. We won't lose another meet with him here."

"But he's so quiet."

"And so unfriendly."

Toby shook his head. "Does anybody really care? I mean, really. What's the difference if he's a mummy? I don't care if he ever says another word or smiles or gets excited and jumps around when we win, lose, or tie. This guy is unbeatable, and he'll give us the state championship. What else matters?"

I was about to say that there were a lot of things that mattered more than that when Cory burst through the door. "Hi, guys! Sorry I'm late. How come Travis was sittin' outside the door? Were you votin' on him or something?"

"That's right! We never voted. Is he still there?"

"No! He was sittin' there when I rode up on my bike, but by

the time I got off and started in here, he was jogging toward his place."

I'm sure Toby felt terrible, but he tried to hide it with a smirk.

5

Marymount

I didn't know whether to pedal right over to Travis's house and talk to him about what he might have heard or just wait until later and let him wonder if I knew he'd been there when we were talking about him.

I decided to go right away because I had to find out if he needed a ride or anything. And I wanted him to know that I would be using him in each of the events he had requested.

When I got to his house, he was mowing the backyard. I parked my bike next to the garage and stood where I knew he could see me. I didn't look directly at him until I was sure he had already seen me, but that proved to be a mistake.

I stood at the end of every row he cut for several minutes, and he never once looked up at me again. We both knew that he knew I was there. So what was this? Should I get mad? Grab him? Shake him? Make him tell me what the trouble was?

Or did I know all too well that he had heard what Toby said? And wouldn't anyone be mad about that? Wouldn't I? But still, a guy has to talk about things. I wanted to know what the trouble was, and he was pretending I wasn't even there.

I was getting madder the longer I stood there with him ignoring me. I couldn't help it. Maybe I owed him an apology, but I didn't know what for. Whatever my friends or I had done wrong, I didn't deserve this. He'd been mean to me this way since the first day he moved in.

I stomped around to the front of the house and banged loudly on the door. His mother answered it without saying anything. "I have a message for Travis."

"He's in the back." Her voice was soft and lazy.

"I know, but he's too busy to talk. I need to tell him something about the track meet."

"He'll be there. I'll bring him."

"Are you sure? He can ride with us. We just live down Baker Street here."

"No, I'll bring him."

"All right. Well, just tell him that I'll use him in all the events he said he wanted to be in, and that he'll also be our leading long jumper. He'll know what that means."

Almost as soon as I'd said that, I wished I hadn't. His mother looked at me as if I'd called her an idiot. To prove she knew just as well as Travis did what track words meant, she summarized the instructions. "So, I'll tell him he's long jumping, running the hundred, the two-twenty, the four-forty, and the mile relay."

"Right. And thank you."

"He ain't gonna like that too very much."

"Pardon me?"

"I say he ain't gonna like that much."

I was stunned. "Why not?"

"I don't believe he wished to long jump."

"But he's the best. I thought he didn't ask to long jump because he didn't want to hog all the events. I'm going to enter him in the long jump, and if he doesn't want to jump, he can pull out."

"If I were you, I wouldn't enter him without his permission."

She was still quiet and soft, but she was clear too. "Thank you, Mrs. Bourne. Tell Travis I'll see him in the morning. You

36

know where the Marymount track is?"

She nodded and shut the door. This sure was a cold family.

The next morning at Marymount, I was leading the Baker Street Sports Club track team in a quarter-mile jog around the all-weather track at Marymount, and we were sneaking peeks at the competition. Marymount had all kinds of kids on their team, but they didn't have nearly the talent we did.

They would put three guys in each track event, but they would not likely win any except a few field events. They were a nice bunch of kids with a good coach and beautiful uniforms and facilities. We always liked running against them.

We were also keeping an eye out for our ace. The meet was to begin at ten, and we had been there since nine-thirty. Soon the Marymount coach, Walter Widder, walked over and thrust out his hand. "Dallas, how've you been? I hear you've got a ringer this year."

"A ringer?"

"Yeah. An outsider. Someone who's going to make you unbeatable, as if you aren't already." He was smiling, and I wasn't ready to unveil our secret weapon yet.

"Who told you that?"

"Oh, a little birdie."

"And did the little birdie give you the name of our outsider? Our ringer?"

"Maybe."

"Well, using an outsider would be against the rules, wouldn't it?"

He nodded, still smiling. "We wouldn't want to see that, Dallas. Especially on the only team that has no adult supervision."

"Mr. Widder, you don't have to worry about us. We play by the rules, and we have no outsider on our team."

"No one from outside your area?"

"No, sir."

"You've not got Travis Bourne on your team, the white-

37

haired kid from the suburbs who scored more points by himself than most of the other *teams* in the state tournament last year?"

"I didn't say that. I said we weren't using anyone from outside our area."

His smile froze. "Don't try to tell me that you've fudged on your boundaries or on where he lives, or that you've got him staying with friends and relatives in your area, because that won't wash. I'll have to write you up. I'd hate to see that happen to your club, Dallas."

If Mr. Widder had been a bad guy, or snotty, or anything like that, I might have let him think that I was lying to him. But he had always been a friend and supporter, which was more than I could say for a lot of the other coaches in the district.

"Mr. Widder, Travis Bourne is on our team. He moved into our neighborhood, and everything is legal."

He sat back and shook his head. "You're putting me on."

"No, sir, I'm not. And I wouldn't."

He clapped me on the shoulder. "I know you wouldn't. But why couldn't he have moved into *my* neighborhood?"

We laughed. I scrambled to get back to my team as he turned away toward his. I had to wait for a runner to pass before I stepped across the track, and only as he jogged past, hood pulled up tight over his white hair, did I realize it was Travis Bourne.

"Travis! You made it! Good to see you!" He kept running. It was maddening. I was beginning to wonder if the guys weren't right. Maybe we *were* better off without a guy who was so cold and sullen and quiet. But still, he would ensure our victory in this meet, hands down.

The field events got started right at ten o'clock, and the first list of winners for the day were all Marymount competitors. Their only two pole vaulters tied for first place at ten feet, two inches.

Toby chided me. "Eight feet would have gotten us third place."

I laughed him off.

Jack finished second in the shot put at forty-nine feet, four inches and first in the javelin at a hundred sixty-nine feet. Toby and Jimmy finished second and third in the discus, both throwing their best distances ever.

Cory was third in the high jump at five-foot six, even though the second place finisher jumped the same height. He had fewer misses during the competition. Going into the long jump competition, we were in sad shape. I was still confident we would win the meet, because we usually trail at the end of the field events and make it up on the track, but we had never trailed this badly before.

The meet was being scored on a five-three-one basis, first place being worth five points, second three, and third one. With Marymount finishing first and second in the pole vault and high jump and our getting only a third place in the high jump, they led 16-1. They finished first and third in the shot put for six more points against our three for Jack's second place. So, they led 22-4. We won the javelin with Jack's good throw, but they picked up four more points with a second and a third, so they led 26-9.

Their five points for a first in the discus was mostly offset by our four points for second and third, but still they led 31-13. The next event was the long jump. We felt fairly confident with Bugsy and Travis going for us.

Except that I couldn't find Travis.

No one seemed to know where he was. He had been warming up all morning, jogging and stretching and sprinting. But now when we needed him, he wasn't around. I had entered him in the long jump without saying anything to him. I knew his mother would have told him.

His mother! Last year she was always at his meets. Surely she wouldn't have simply dropped him off and left. I looked for her in the stands. I finally located her near the top of the far end of the bleachers all by herself. That's when I remembered that I had seen her before. She had been at the meets last year with two little girls. I wondered whatever happened to them. And their father.

He had been at the meets too. He was always in the infield, even though he wasn't a coach or a photographer. He had a way of weaseling his way onto the track and shouting at his son during a meet. But he wasn't here today.

Bugsy was the first competitor called for the long jump. He fouled on his first attempt. That was rare for Bugsy, and I assumed it was because he wanted to do better than he ever had before, better even than Travis Bourne.

Meanwhile, I was looking for Travis.

On his second attempt, Bugsy jumped sixteen and a half feet, an incredible performance for a twelve-year-old. The Marymount jumpers were doing fairly well, but they weren't in Bugsy's class. A first place would be nice in the event, and we would outscore our opponents five to four, but that wouldn't be enough, trailing by as much as we were.

We needed a first and a second to bring the score to 32-21. Then we would be within striking distance. But to do that, I would have to find Travis Bourne. His name was on the list as a competitor in the long jump, and the officials were calling for him.

"Second call for Bourne, Travis. Bourne!"

6

Change of Plans

When the officials made their third and final call for "Bourne, Travis," I scrambled up the bleachers toward his mother.

"Do you know where he is?" I was shouting. She just nodded and pointed. I looked back down to the long jump pit. He was there, slowly taking off his sweats.

"I tol' you he probably wouldn't want to long jump. He's not ready."

"What's that mean?"

"Just that he was gonna concentrate on runnin' this year, that's all. Long jumpin' is hard on the body, you know. Dangerous too."

"How long can he jump? I don't recall from last year."

"He's been over seventeen feet."

I ignored her remark about the danger. "Good. That's just what we need."

I turned and ran down to watch him, only then remembering that I had forgotten to thank or say good-bye to his mother. Oh, well, the way she—and he—had been treating me lately, what was the difference?

I wanted to encourage Travis in the long jump, but by the time I slid into position on the grass to watch, he was at the line. Saying anything then would have interrupted his concentration, and I didn't want that. No way. We needed every point he could give us now.

Travis ran easily down the runway and slowed before getting to the takeoff spot. Then he trotted back to the line and began rocking back and forth. But when he took off again, even though it was clear he would not stop and come back again, he was not running much faster than he had for the practice run.

I recalled in the state meet the year before when he had exploded down the runway, putting all his sprinting speed into it, then transferring that horizontal speed into both horizontal and vertical power and finishing second in the state.

He loped toward the takeoff, and I knew that at that speed he would be able to jump only a dozen or so feet, even with the best technique. But he didn't even jump. He ran right through the pit. His takeoff foot had hit the spot just right, but he kept running. Of course, with his running so slowly, it didn't mean anything that his takeoff foot landed in the right spot, because at a higher speed he would take fewer steps and would have to worry even more about foot placement.

"Foul!" The red flag shot up and for his first of three attempts. Travis was given a "no distance."

By the time I got to Travis, he was sitting on the ground with his sweat pants draped over his legs and his knees drawn up. He lowered his head and hid his face between his knees, covering himself with his sweat shirt. He didn't look upset or tired. He was just relaxed and quiet.

I clapped him on the back. "Just gettin' the feel of the runway? I noticed you didn't practice earlier."

Nothing.

"You're OK, aren't you? I mean, you're not hurt or anything?"

He shook his head.

"Gonna jump again, of course?"

He nodded.

"Good. I'm gonna watch Bugsy."

44

Bugsy jumped about fifteen-and-a-half feet, which is more within his range. It would have placed him second, had it not been for his great first leap. I told Travis how badly we needed a good performance from him. "Just do something that will make Bugsy second, and we'll cop eight points from this event."

When Travis was called again, he sighed, shed his sweats, and ambled to the line. He ran much more swiftly down the runway this time, and when he hit the takeoff mark, he lifted gracefully in a low arc, not his usually flashy fashion. Still, the jump carried him more than sixteen feet, just short of Bugsy's mark.

It was not what I expected, but it was what we wanted. Barring an incredibly unusual jump by one of the Marymount competitors, we would have our one-two finish and eight points.

As soon as he was out of the pit, Travis grabbed his sweats and hurried off with them under his arms. I yelled congratulations and encouragement to him, but he didn't act as if he heard, and I couldn't get close enough to really talk to him.

I hadn't figured on Bugsy's next jump. I told him to take it easy and save himself for the quarter and the half, but he wouldn't even hear of it.

"Are you kidding? I might be able to jump seventeen feet! I've never felt this good or jumped this far before. Anyway, if I *don't* improve on my first jump, Travis is gonna beat me, and my best jump ever will wind up as a second place!"

But he overdid it. He stumbled before taking off and tumbled into the asphalt before the pit, scraping elbows and knees and shoulders and rolling over and over in the sand. He was in pain as we hustled him off to the showers to wash the dirt from his wounds, which didn't appear serious.

By the time he was out of the showers and had a few bandages applied, however, it was clear he had also injured his knee. He was limping and wouldn't be running any more that day. I didn't know what to do about the half mile. I knew

45

Travis could win the quarter, but now I would probably have to put Ryan in the half as well as the mile.

That was a lot to expect from him, especially now that I would likely need him back in the mile relay for a quarter too. I headed back out to the long jump pit to see how Travis had done on his last attempt.

An official gave me the word. "Your man scratched his last jump."

"What do you mean?"

"Didn't show. Still finished second though. Baker Street gets one and two, Marymount three."

That meant we trailed 32-21 going into the track events. With Bugsy, we were sure winners. With a makeshift team now, only Travis could pull it out for us. And who knew where he was?

I knew one thing, I had had it. Even if it caused Travis to drop out of the meet and off the team and cost us the meet and the state championship and everything else, I was going to have it out with him and right then.

All I wanted to do was find him and scold him and let him know that he was not the only person on this team. I was the captain, and I had everyone else to think of. No one in our club decides what he will or will not enter or what he will or will not scratch.

The problem was, of course, that the scolding I went over in my mind would not be so clear and forceful when I *did* find him. I wasn't sure I could talk to anyone that way. I was mad enough to, and if he irritated me any more, I was going to let him have it with both barrels.

He did. When I found him, I started out nice. "Thanks for helping us win the long jump. First and second was what we wanted. Couldn't you have beaten Bugsy though?"

He shrugged.

"How come you scratched on the third jump?"

He shrugged again, and that did it.

"Travis, I've taken this silent treatment of yours for just about long enough, wouldn't you say? Can't you just answer a simple question? I mean, I know you're great, probably the best in the state and maybe even the country, but what did we do to deserve this kind of treatment? I want to know why you scratched in the long jump, and I want to know now."

He stared at me, his eyes on fire. "You got your first and second place in the long jump, didn't you?"

I was stunned. It was the most he had said to me for ages. I nodded.

"Then leave me alone. I didn't want to long jump anyway. I can jump eighteen feet, but all you needed was sixteen, and that's what I gave you. Now back off."

He walked away.

My face was red, and my ears were burning. I kept telling myself that if I had any self respect I would chase him down and throw him off the team for talking to me like that. But I was too embarrassed. Anyway, we needed him.

I didn't want him terrorizing me or the rest of the guys or making up his own rules for himself the rest of the season, but I decided I would have to wait until after this meet to worry about that.

We would need a first, second, and third in the hundred to get back into the meet. I was only a little surprised to see Travis in the starting blocks, one lane over from Brent. I was on the far inside lane as I settled in and leaned forward to press my fingers and thumb onto the starting line.

Travis was still working with his blocks. He set them strangely, the block for the left foot way up at the front, the block for the right all the way to the back. Everyone else set theirs fairly close together, but Travis knelt in his usual style with his left knee near his face and his right leg way back behind him.

At the sound of the starter's pistol, Travis drove that left foot against the block and swung his trailing right leg out in front of him in a flash. He was five feet ahead of the rest of us in the first instant, and by the fifty-yard mark he appeared to be gliding away from us.

I was dead even with Brent, and the slower Marymount sprinters were far behind us. Usually I was able to outrun Brent, but Travis's unusual style and speed sapped some of my concentration and somehow just made Brent that much more determined. His head and eyes were straight ahead, as if he was ignoring the leader.

I was watching him too, but I found it distracting. With twenty-five yards to go, I knew I was going to finish third for the first time in my life if I didn't get moving. I tucked my chin down and drove for all I was worth.

As I crossed the finish line I realized that I had passed not just Brent, but also Travis. And even Brent had passed Travis. He must have slowed down at the end because he was able to stop just past the finish line in third place.

What in the world was going on? We had swept the event, but we'd be sunk if Travis was hurt too.

7

Fight to the Finish

Well, Travis hadn't been hurt. Cory told me that he had watched the entire race and that just as Brent and I seemed to really be going head to head, Travis just slowed up and let us pass him, making sure only that he finished ahead of the Marymount runners.

I wanted to talk to Travis about it, but once again he wasn't around. I wondered if he had been this much trouble in his suburban team the year before.

An hour later, the same three of us were lined up for the two-twenty. Marymount had entered only two runners in the race, and they were the ones who had finished fifth and sixth in the hundred. We weren't worried, but I was curious about how Travis would handle this race.

He set up his starting blocks the same as he had the time before. At the gun, however, he didn't start the same way. He didn't explode out of the blocks. He just seemed to roll out and stay right with me the first half of the race. Then I lost sight of him. He was drifting back!

I knew he was faster than I was, but I could see Brent on my left and no one else. Travis was back to my right somewhere. I just hoped he wouldn't mess around so much that he let one of the Marymount guys catch him.

That was unlikely, but still I didn't like all this horseplay.

Suddenly Travis shot past me. Much as I wanted to win, that made me feel better. But then he started drifting again, just loping along. Brent and I caught him again and went past. When he took the lead again, I realized he was just toying with us. We exchanged the lead two more times, then we finished with me first, Brent second, and Travis third.

Exhausted and out of breath, I grabbed Travis before he could get away. I demanded an explanation. "What was that all about?" He shrugged and turned away, but I caught his shirt. "No, I want to know!"

"What're you talkin' about, O'Neil? You got your first, second, and third, didn't you?"

"But you could have won that race! You could have won both of them! And you could have won the long jump too! What's going on?"

He didn't turn away, but he didn't say anything either. He just stared me down. "You're up in the quarter alone. Can you pull it off, or are you going to horse that one up too?"

"If you don't want me in it, just say so."

What could I say? Of course I wanted him in it. I walked off, shaking my head. He won the quarter by a long way, but of course Marymount finished second and third. With the nine point sweep of the hundred and the five-four edge in the quarter, we led 43-36 with only the half, the mile, and the mile relay to go.

The half mile really had me buffaloed. I had no idea who to put in it. No one wanted to run it, myself included, and Travis couldn't because he was already entered in the maximum number of events. Finally, I entered.

It was foolish. I wasn't trained for the half mile, and even the thought of trying to run eight hundred eighty yards in competition turned my stomach.

I started out strong enough and in fact was leading at the end of the first quarter mile. Then it hit me. I couldn't breathe, couldn't get my legs to move normally, couldn't gain any speed. I was tying up the way I had seen too many distance runners do in the past.

On the backstretch, a Marymount runner passed me so fast I knew I would never catch him. He pulled away and looked excited about what would probably be his first victory ever. I glanced behind me, which you're not supposed to do, and saw another gaining on me.

I didn't want him to pass me. After all this work and pain and agony, a third place would give us only one point. I tried to calculate what a first and a second would do for Marymount, but I was too whipped to think.

With a hundred yards to go, the second Marymount runner came pounding up behind me. I lifted my arms as high as I could on each swing and tried to force my legs to follow, but I couldn't hold him off. He chugged past me, and I relaxed, knowing I couldn't catch him.

A third place! That was all I was going to get. Well, one point was better than nothing. But with fifty yards to go, and me hardly moving, yet another runner came up behind me. I didn't have the strength to turn and look, but I knew it had to be an opponent. Baker Street didn't have anyone else in the race.

As the footsteps got closer, I searched deep within myself to see if there was anything more I could muster to hold him off. I didn't think there was, but the thought of running a half mile with nothing to show for it—not even one point—was something I just couldn't bear.

I threw my head back and gave it everything I had. The Marymount runner drew even with me, and we staggered toward the finish line together, gasping for breath. It was as if we were running in place, the two leaders still pulling away.

Then they had finished. It was just the third Marymount runner and me, and the crowd was screaming. Their first place had given them five points, second place another three. That gave them 44 points to our 43. Third place would put them two points up, later in a meet than they had ever led before.

I fought and fought and just when I thought I was too tied up to move anymore and was about to pass out, we stumbled past the finish line. I had edged him by a half step. We had earned a big point, and the score was tied at 44.

I never wanted to run a half mile again as long as I lived. All I could think of was that I had run a similar race against Travis Bourne the first night we had met. From then on, all I wanted to do was run a half mile easy for a workout. Never again in competition.

Yet, when I began to get my breath back and cool down, I felt pretty good. I was satisfied with my effort, even though I had only barely broken three minutes. As I slowly walked around, getting my legs back, I noticed Ryan looking very worried before the start of the mile.

Ryan was a kind of mathematician, and he had been figuring all the scoring and potential scoring. "You realize I'm our only entry in this race, Dallas?"

I nodded. "Just like I was in the half."

"But if I do as bad in this as you did in that, we can't win the meet."

"As bad? I did the best I could, man! If I hadn't held off that third guy, we'd be behind right now!"

"I know. But you finished third. I'm telling you that if I finish third, we get one point, they get first and second for eight points, and then even if we win the relay, we only outscore them five to three, and they win."

"So, what if you finish second?"

"We still lose automatically!"

"Even before the relay?"

"Yup! Unless they don't finish. If they finish at all, they get three for the relay, but if I finish second in the mile, we go into the relay with forty-seven. They would get five points for first and one for third, giving them six points for a total of fifty going into the relay.

"Then, even if we win the relay and outscore them five to three, they win fifty-three to fifty-two."

"So, you have to win the mile, Ryan."

"Thanks a lot."

I didn't blame him anymore for looking so worried. "You know, even if you win it, we still have to win the relay to win the meet. If you outscore 'em five to four and they outscore us five to three, they win."

He shook his head. "How am I supposed to save anything for the mile relay if I am forced to win the mile?"

"Don't worry about the relay, Ryan. If you don't win the mile, the relay doesn't make any difference anyway."

After all that worrying and figuring and carrying on, Ryan had no trouble winning the mile. Their second and third place runners were so far back that Ryan was able to slow almost to a walk for the last quarter, winning with his slowest time in two years.

At the end he said he felt great, but of course our lead was just one point at 49-48, because Marymount runners had finished second and third. The winners of the relay would get five points, the losers three, if they finished. That gave Marymount the perfect opportunity for a dramatic upset, especially since one of our top guys was out with a knee injury.

Normally, I would lead off the mile relay with Ryan second, Brent third, and Bugsy fourth. With Travis on the team, I was going to stay first, put Brent second, Bugsy third, and Travis fourth. Now, with Bugsy out, I put Brent back in for him, allowing Ryan the longest time to wait after his mile race.

The trouble was, I didn't realize how much my half mile run had taken out of me. I had recovered quickly, but that was just for survival. To run again, and hard, for four hundred forty yards? I thought I had it in me, but I didn't.

I started quickly, racing to a big lead at the one-hundred yard mark, but all of a sudden my thighs and calves were knotted up. My heart was slamming in my chest, and my breath was already gone. I was fighting to hang on, and I wasn't even halfway around the track yet.

At the two-twenty point, the Marymount leadoff man drew up to me. I didn't want to appear too beat, so I tried to retain my composure. Nothing doing. He eased by, and I couldn't fight him off. I saw the second men on each team switch positions (the first place team gets the inside lane for the handoff).

I knew I had to stay as close as possible to give our team a chance to win. Brent would normally have been our slowest man in this event, had Ryan not just run a mile. But now he was probably second fastest, because I was certainly not showing well. I was behind by at least fifteen yards when I passed him the baton and collapsed in the infield.

I didn't even have the strength to watch. They would be coming around the far turn before their handoffs, so I decided I would pick them up there when I could muster some interest in what was going on. For now, I'd rather have been asleep or dead for all the pain it caused just to breathe.

8

The Outcome

When the number two runner from Marymount came dashing around the far curve toward the starting line for the next handoff, I wondered if Brent had dropped out. He was nowhere in sight.

I sat up and whirled around. He was still on the track but looked to be about a hundred yards behind. "C'mon, Brent! Get closer! We need it! You can do it!"

Fortunately, the Marymount runner was running out of gas too. His face was white and his eyes vacant as he made the slow, sloppy handoff. Brent made up about twenty yards with a clean handoff and a strong finish to his leg of the relay.

Marymount's third man settled into his pace a little too quickly, because Ryan was on the run. He tried to make up too much of the ground too soon, and although he was successful at first—closing to within about thirty yards—from there he had to settle for just not letting his opponent get any farther head.

Clearly, none of the Marymount runners were comfortable with the quarter mile. Their anchorman was the best they had, and he took off like a shot, which is more than I can say for Travis. Several seconds later, Travis took the baton and casually looked up the track to see how much ground he had to make up.

He started slowly and ran easily, and I was so mad at him I couldn't even yell. I just stood and watched as he slowly loped through the first two hundred twenty yards, fully thirty feet behind their man.

Then, as if shot from a cannon, Travis took off. He broke into that smooth, hardly-touching-the-ground style of his and began floating toward the lead. He came up so fast on the Marymount man that his opponent looked first over one shoulder, then the other, and nearly stumbled trying to keep the lead.

He sped up as much as he could, but it was virtually over when Travis blew by him. I thought he would bury the man, but he slowed and stayed just a couple of steps ahead of him. It looked crazy to me. What if it made the Marymount man mad, and he found some strength to finish hard?

He tried, but Travis had enough left to hold him off. He won by a couple of steps, hardly breathing hard. He had made up the difference, settled in in front of the man, and had expended only the effort necessary to win. And I realized he had done the same thing all day long.

The question was why? Didn't he enjoy blowing people away, showing off, setting new records? Apparently not, but the year before he certainly had.

Our whole team gathered around to slap high fives and congratulate each other, but of course we wanted Travis most of all. He had made the difference. We were going to hoist him on our shoulders and parade him around a bit, but—needless to say—we couldn't find him or his mother.

He and I had had words with each other. We said some cross things. Did that mean he wouldn't be back? That he would return the uniform and forget about us? Or did he see how much fun winning could be and that we would take him to the state finals again, maybe in a bigger way than his suburban team had the year before?

I tried to push all the negative thoughts from my mind on our way home. I knew that if Bugsy was healthy—and his knee injury proved to be minor and temporary—we had enough strength to qualify for the state meet easily. With Travis, of course.

And if we could win three events while a couple of the rest of us finished second or third in ours, we would win the state team crown. It seemed to be hoping for an awful lot, but we wanted to shoot for nothing less.

Cory sat next to me in the car and asked if he and Jimmy could talk to me when we got home.

"Sure. What about?"

"Travis."

I nodded, wondering what they wanted. Probably, like everyone else, they just wanted to make sure we kept him happy and kept him on the team. At that moment, I was even willing to put up with his irritating silent behavior and all the funny business on the track if it meant we would keep winning.

Some of the other guys didn't think so. Both Toby and Ryan were mad at Travis. "Who does he think he is, fooling around like that? You wouldn't put up with that from any of the rest of us, Dallas. Why did you put up with it from him?"

I turned to face them. "I didn't, really. I told him off after the two-twenty, and he went out and won the four-forty going away."

"Yeah, but then he pulls that stunt in the mile relay. You think maybe he just slowed down because he was tired from catching the guy? Or was he really just showing off?"

"Neither. I think he was doing only what he had to do to win."

"But why?"

I didn't know, so I didn't try to say.

Toby was outspoken. "I think he oughta be off the team."

Ryan agreed. "I'm not sure he's *on* the team yet! We haven't voted him into the club."

That made me mad. "OK, you want to vote right now? You want to think first about how we'd be feeling right now if

61

he hadn't won that meet for us? He scored three points in the long jump, a point in the hundred, another one in the two-twenty, five in the four-forty, and without him we wouldn't have won five in the mile relay. Chalk up fifteen big ones out of our fifty-four."

That shut them up for a while, and we avoided the vote. I was sure the vote would have gone against Travis just then, because we require a unanimous vote on new members. We don't want anyone in the club that everyone doesn't agree on.

Everyone but Cory and Jimmy and I split up and went home when they got to my house. We threw our gear aside and walked out by the corral. We were all tired but feeling good about having won. At least I was. Jimmy and Cory looked like they had something heavy on their minds.

"So, which side do you guys come down on, in or out?"

"What're you talking about, Dallas?"

"I just want to know if you want Travis in or out."

Jimmy spoke, "In, of course."

Cory nodded. "But that's not what we want to talk about."

What he had said didn't really register with me until I had started in with my own comment. "Me too. I mean this guy is something else. He can carry us a long way. He makes me mad, yeah, just like he does everyone else, but I'm glad you agree that we're better off with him than without him. I can't let him take over or make up his own rules, and some things are going to have to change, but he's worth it. Hey, what do you mean that's not what you wanted to talk about?"

Jimmy thrust his hands into his pockets and leaned back against a fence post. "We want to talk about acting like a Christian. We've learned a lot from you about that, Dallas, and—"

"Hey, you can't expect Travis to act like a Christian until he is one, and we don't have any reason to believe that he is."

"We're not talking about him. And anyway, do we have any reason to believe that he isn't?"

I pawed at the ground with my toe. "His mother swears. I heard her."

"So does mine."

"Mine too."

I got the point. Both Jimmy and Cory had become Christians and started going to church with me even though their parents didn't agree. I shrugged, then nodded. "I just don't think he is, that's all."

Cory tried. "What we're getting at, Dallas, is this: have you prayed for Travis Bourne?"

"You bet I have. Every day. And you've heard me." We still had devotions together every morning.

"We've heard you pray that Travis would join the sports club and the track team, yeah. But is that praying for Travis or praying for the team?"

Jimmy squinted and shook his head. "Or is that praying for yourself, Dal?"

He said it as kindly as he could, and it seemed he'd had to muster a lot of courage to do it, but still it offended me. I was hurt, and it probably showed. I got a little defensive. "So now I'm selfish? Who do you guys think you are, criticizing the way I pray?"

"We'd want you to criticize us if you thought we needed it. And we have. And you have."

Cory was smiling. Jimmy wasn't. He had seen me like this before, and it wasn't pleasant. He didn't want me to get so mad that I missed the point. He took over to try to soothe me. "All we're saying, Dallas, is that we look up to you. We watch you. We learn from you. We didn't know anything about being Christians and praying and reading the Bible and memorizing verses and all that. You're kind of like our model for that stuff."

I nodded, uncomfortable. I was still smarting. "Yeah, so?"

"So we're wondering if we're supposed to act the way you act toward Travis? We don't think so, and we wanted to tell you that and see what you thought."

"Well, I got mad at Travis because I'm supposed to be in charge of the team and the club, and he was acting pretty independent. That's my job, to keep people in line. It's not yours, so if it bothers you, you don't have to do it anyway."

Jimmy and Cory whispered to each other and that really got me mad. "Now you guys are talking about me right in front of me?"

Cory tried to explain. "I was just sayin' that you're not getting the point. We're talking about your frustration with Travis. We're all frustrated with him. And we don't want your job as leader of the club either.

"It's just that you didn't want the job as captain of the team when you first got it, and that's what made you so good at it. You weren't showing off, making a big deal of being in charge."

"And now I am?"

"A little. Only since Travis has been around and challenging you some. It's like, now we have a chance to really have an impressive, state championship team, and you need to make sure everybody knows who's behind it."

"But I'm *not* behind it! All the guys are! And Travis is the key. I know that. He'll get all the credit he deserves. He's gonna make us what we will be."

Cory ran a freckly hand through his shock of rusty, red hair. "OK, all that was just a smokescreen to find out where you were on Travis. Now I need to really tell you what we're thinking."

"You haven't already?"

"Hardly."

"Let 'er rip."

And they did.

9

Right Between the Eyes

Cory began. "Before I tell you this, Dallas, I want to say that we've all been guilty. At least most of us."

I was still on the defensive. I sighed. "All of who?"

"All of us in the Baker Street Sports Club. It's not just you."

"It's not just me doing what?"

Cory cocked his head. "Treating Travis Bourne like a piece of meat."

I was nearly speechless. "Wha—?"

"No, just be quiet for a minute and listen to me, Dallas. From the first day he moved in, all any of us wanted was to get him into our club and onto our team. Who wouldn't? There's nothing wrong with that.

"But it was also obvious, right from the beginning, that there's trouble at the Bourne house or at least in their family. We all remember his father, who used to show up for every meet and badger Travis and yell for him and at him. He seemed to be real interested in the kid, but they didn't seem close. You remember that?"

I nodded.

"And remember we used to see his mother and a couple of little sisters around all the time, usually up in the stands? They were about the age of your sisters."

I nodded again.

"Well, think. They move into our area, but no father and no two daughters. Something's up, Dallas. You had to wonder about it."

"Yeah, I did, but—"

Jimmy interrupted me with a raised hand and let Cory keep talking. "OK, you wondered about it, just like we all did. But which one of us asked him?"

"He wouldn't even say hello, let alone let me ask—"

"Let me finish. You may have tried, I don't know. But all you ever said to us, all you ever talked about, and all you ever said to him centered around what he could do for us and our team. He's a hunk of meat to you, Dal. You wanted him on the team for his talent, not for himself or what we could do for him."

I wanted to argue, to say it wasn't true, but Cory had me. A new, growing Christian, one I was supposed to be bringing along, had me right between the eyes. "You saw the beauty of having the best athlete in the state on our team, in our club, and you didn't care what his problems were, why he was living with only his mother and not the rest of his family.

"All you cared about was getting him in the club. When he didn't seem interested and was so quiet, you figured he was just a strange guy. The problem was, *you* had become a strange guy. I know that sounds terrible, but you haven't been yourself lately, Dal. Even when you worked up the courage to tell him off, you were protecting your position and not finding out what his problem was. Demanding to know what was going on didn't make him any more open to talk. In fact, he just got surly. That was worse."

I sat on the ground and hung my head. I was through arguing. They had me. "I feel terrible."

Jimmy lumbered down next to me. "We wanted to talk to you about it, Dallas, because we knew you were a good guy and could take it. For a while we thought we'd just let you come to your senses by yourself. But it seemed to be getting worse. Yes, there are some things that Travis is doing that

68

you can't let him do, even if he wins us the track championship of the Milky Way. But first, you've got to get next to him and find out what's going on.

"How do you think he feels, being assigned to carry our team? You had him long jumping on a message from his mother. It's no wonder he was just doing what you asked and nothing more. It's a wonder he even ran in the meet. He loves track and field and wants to stay in shape and compete statewide. But I think it's clear he doesn't really want to be on this team where everybody—especially the leader—just sees him as a lock on the state championship."

I clasped my hands together. "I suppose you expected more from me."

Cory spoke again. "We still think the world of you, Dallas. But, yes, of course we did. You've always been the one who leads the way in being sensitive to people, in knowing what to say. You can cool guys down, put them in their places, build them up, whatever they need. Yet you haven't done that with Travis. That's all we wanted to say. We know you'll take care of it."

"And you guys will pray for me?"

"We always do."

That evening after supper, I rode my bike to Travis Bourne's house. He and his mother were sitting in the living room, watching television. I knocked.

"Can Travis be interrupted? I want to talk with him outside if it's all right."

He came out slowly, without looking at me, and sat on the steps.

I sat on the ground below him. I pulled a blade of grass and chewed it as I spoke. "I owe you a big apology, Travis."

He looked quickly at me, almost as if he was about to speak. I hadn't ever had to worry about his interrupting me! "No, I do, Travis. All I could think of when I found out you moved in here was what you could do for the Baker Street

69

Sports Club track team. What you could do for me, really. I treated you like something other than just another kid who happens to have a lot of talent. I didn't care about you or what might be going on in your life. I never even asked you why you moved in here.

"As I think back on how I talked to you, it makes me embarrassed. I mean, I guess it's understandable that I would act the way I did. You might even have done the same thing if you were me and a great athlete moved it. But it wasn't right, and I'm sorry, and I want you to forgive me."

At first I could hardly believe I had got all that out. I had planned to say a lot more, but I got flustered and just said what came to me. I was afraid he was going to just get up and go back in the house, because this couldn't be any easier for him than it was for me.

"I *did* feel like a prize."

"I know, and I can understand that. I'm sorry."

"You don't have to keep apologizing, Dallas. It's all right."

"No, it isn't. I was stupid and selfish, and—"

"Please. It's all right. I understand."

"Well, I really do want your forgiveness, and if you want to tell me, I want to know about you and your family and your move and anything else you think is any of my business."

He reached down and grabbed a handful of grass, then let it drift from his fingers in the wind. When he finally spoke again, it was soft and flat. "My dad's in jail. My sisters are in foster homes. It's tearin' up me and my mama."

I felt ashamed, but more than that, I felt so sorry for him I wanted to cry. I was also curious, of course, but I wasn't about to ask any more questions. Not about something like that. That was stuff a guy would tell you only if he felt like it. I wouldn't have blamed him if he hadn't. But he did.

"He was a child abuser. We could never make him happy. I did everything I could to please him. I wanted to be the best there ever was at everything I did, but the only thing I could do was run and jump. I couldn't hit a baseball, I couldn't throw a strike, I couldn't shoot a basketball. But I could run. And so I ran. But you know what he said to me after last year's state meet when I took two firsts and two seconds as an eleven-year-old? He said if I wasn't so lazy I would have had four firsts."

I didn't know what to say. Are you supposed to agree with a guy when he's saying his father is a creep? I wondered what had caused his father to be that way, and I'm sure Travis had wondered too, but I wasn't going to ask. He sort of answered it anyway.

"He's a pretty hard drinker and had trouble keepin' jobs. My ma worked a lot. Still does. But when he started hurtin' the girls, that was it for me. I decided I wouldn't take it anymore. I would stand up to him. Got my lip busted pretty good, but then my ma turned him in. She had stories that wouldn't quit, stuff I hadn't even known about. When I heard all that, I was glad they sent him up, but we never expected to lose the girls. The judge said that with Ma havin' to work, they'd have to be taken care of by someone else. Breaks our hearts, and it's all his fault."

Suddenly it was as silent as a graveyard, like we were mourning someone's death. In a way I guess we were. A family had been put out of its misery, only to find itself sadder than ever. When I thought of how I treated this boy and his mother when they were going through such pain, I could have dug a hole and buried myself. He didn't want me to apologize anymore, so I didn't. But I wished I could have.

He didn't say anything for the longest time, and there was nothing coming to my mind. In a way I wanted to say something about hoping he would still be on the team and then just leave and go home. But something else made me want to sit there with him all night.

He needed a friend, and the reason I wanted him to stay on the team was because I knew the other guys would make a friend of him if he'd let them. I didn't want to push him, I didn't want to make him out our only hope for the future or anything like that. Most of all, I didn't want to make him feel like he had to be perfect to please me or my teammates or anyone else.

He shook his head and sighed. "You'll never know how good it felt to finish wherever I wanted to today and then to basically tell you to drop dead when you didn't like it. That's not the kind of person I am, Dallas, but it felt so good to have a little control and to not be doing just what everybody wanted me too. I just can't tell you how that made me feel."

I nodded and said I understood. And I did. "I need you to forgive me, Travis. I won't apologize anymore because I know you don't like that, but I feel terrible, and I want you to let me start making it right. I'll never treat you like a prize or a piece of meat or anything except a person again. I want to be your friend, and I want you to be mine. But you've got to forgive me."

Travis looked real uncomfortable and didn't say anything for the longest time. He shifted his weight, grabbed some more grass, chewed some, and let some fly. Then he stood and turned, then turned back and sat down again. I couldn't see any tears, but I could hear them in his voice.

"This is gonna sound pretty stupid, Dallas. But I've never forgiven anyone for anything before, and I guess I'm not sure how you do it."

I nodded to show I knew what he was talking about. "Well, I'm just saying—well, you know what I'm saying about how I feel about what I did to you, how I treated you, and all that. And all I want from you is to know that you heard and understood and that you're not going to hold it against me."

"Oh, I would never do that."

"Then if you'll just tell me you forgive me and that you're willing to let me try again to be your friend, that's all there is to it."

"That's forgiveness? Just not holding it against you and telling you so?"

"That's it, and believe me, I need it."

72

He stuck out his hand and shook mine. "You've got it, Dallas."

"Call me Dal. My friends do."

"OK, Dal."

10

On to State!

The change in Travis Bourne and his attitude toward the Baker Street Sports Club was almost too good to be true. He was still sort of quiet but not moody, not distant, not sullen.

He was a friendly, shy sort of a guy who enjoyed sharing his knowledge. And he had a lot of it. The guys, myself included, started looking to him almost as a coach. There were reasons he did what he did on the track, and as he shared what he had learned from books and from experimenting, we all improved.

The guys looked forward to our daily workouts, and we saw times improving in every event. Bugsy's improvement was probably the most dramatic, as his times came down drastically in the quarter and the half, and his distances were increased in the long jump.

His injuries had healed nicely, and he was hoping to be a medalist in the state tournament. There were several dual and triangular and quadrangular meets before that, but our team was getting so good, we started looking to those as mere tune-ups for the big one at the end of the month.

Travis had some strategy for one of the big quad meets a couple of weeks before the state finals. "We should move our guys around a little, let them specialize in something other than their top events. We may finish second or third in this meet instead of first, but that will only make the winner feel overconfident at the state finals. In fact, it'll take some of the spotlight off us from other parts of the state where they may have heard about us already."

We tried it. Several of the sprinters tried the weight events. Did we do horribly! Then we put Jack and Toby on the mile relay team. They had to time us with a calendar! But everyone had fun. It was a great meet for relaxation and morale.

Meanwhile, Jimmy and Cory and I were praying earnestly for Travis. We wanted to be able to talk to him about Jesus and to let him know that God had forgiveness available for him and his family, and yes, even his father.

Jimmy invited Travis to Sunday school with us, and I was shocked when he not only said yes but also added that his mother would be bringing him and staying with him for church. "She's a churchgoer from way back. Only she hasn't gone for years. She's lookin' forward to it."

That gave me the courage to ask Travis if he'd like to meet with Jimmy and Cory and me every morning for a story, some Bible reading, a memory verse, and prayer.

He didn't seem interested. "I don't think so, Dallas. Not just yet."

"Whenever you're ready."

"Well, I'm real interested in what we're learnin' in church and everything, but prayin' in front of people and readin' the Bible, I don't know."

I didn't want to push him. I figured he'd come around eventually. Meanwhile, we'd just keep seeing him at church for as long as he'd come, and we would mention it to him casually if he missed a Sunday. "We missed you."

He hardly ever missed, and when he did he either told us in advance or had a good excuse. Our Sunday school teacher asked if we were working on getting him into our daily devotional group. "We sure are. Why?"

"I just think it would be good for him. He doesn't seem to

76

understand fully what it means to believe and receive Christ, and I think if he was meeting with you boys every day, he might. That should be our next goal in prayer and action. Getting Travis to join you guys every day."

Travis had his own goals. He wanted to see us run away—literally—with the state championship. From my experience, I knew that he was the only one among us who really had a shot at a first place in the state, and he might take as many as four.

He kept saying that he thought there were two other events in which we had a chance, but he wouldn't say which ones. At first I wondered if he might have his eye on both Toby and Ryan because their attitudes had changed so dramatically towards him. But in timing and measuring them in practice, I knew their efforts were not even close to blue ribbon quality for the state meet.

The most exciting dual meet we had before the state finals was against Travis's former team, the Kane County Cougars. It was the perfect tune-up for the state meet because it was held at the Kane County Junior College stadium, where the state meet would be held a week later.

They had beautiful facilities. The track was rubberized asphalt and as fast as they came. The runways for long jumping and pole vaulting were long and didn't interrupt any other running surface. The field events were inside the stadium but far enough from the track not to interfere. It couldn't have been nicer if we were in the olympics.

Travis thought that we shouldn't mess around in this meet. "This one is for blood. This will show how we'll do in the state meet. All our times and distances will show us where we should finish next week."

The Cougars were tough, and of course, they were out for revenge since they'd lost their best runner to us. They were friendly, though, and most of them greeted Travis warmly. The Cougars had nice white uniforms with diagonal, purple stripes across the front.

Jack put the shot a little over fifty feet on the first throw and passed his next two efforts to see if it would hold up. We all knew he could throw farther, but he had been having some trouble with his back, so we let him wait. It was the wrong choice. A Cougar beat him by inches on his last throw, and Jack finished second.

That was too bad, because in a meet against a team that had plenty of entrants in each event, the few guys we had competing all had to win as many firsts as possible.

Jack also finished second in the javelin, but Toby and Jimmy finished first and second in the discus. Cory's high jump placed him third for just one point, and suddenly we were trailing Kane County 21-15.

Travis and Bugsy finished first and second in the long jump to put us up 23-22, but Kane swept the pole vault and the nine points pushed them up to 31-23. We felt confident in the sprints, and, sure enough, Travis won both the hundred and the two-twenty. The only problem was, I finished fourth and Brent fifth in each, so the five points we got from Travis were the only ones we got in those events.

Travis won the quarter, with Bugsy third, so that put us within three points of Kane at 42-39. The surprise of the day came when Bugsy won the half mile, but that gave us only a five-four edge, because he was our only half miler. Now we trailed 46-44.

Ryan won the mile with a five-minute-and-thirty-second run, but they finished second and third, so we were still down 51-49. It all came down to the mile relay again. The winner would get five, the loser three. To win the meet, we had to win the relay.

I was stunned to see that the first leg of the relay would be run by the man who had finished second in the open quarter for Kane. Usually a team puts its best man last, but here I would be facing their best.

He was super. Travis had just nipped him at the tape in his best time ever, and both of them could outrun me by ten seconds over that distance. This man had run Bugsy into the ground, and Bugsy could beat me easily in the quarter.

Travis and the rest kept encouraging me, but I was sick. I just couldn't see how I could even keep us in the race having to face that guy right off the bat.

We were off with the gun, and it was clear I was unprepared. I couldn't get comfortable, and when I finally did, I realized I had settled into much too slow a pace. Their man was pulling away quickly, and it was all I could do to hang on.

By the end of my leg, I had put us behind so far I was sure we could never catch up. Brent took the baton and didn't allow them to get any farther ahead, but there was a sloppy exchange with Bugsy, and we fell back another five yards or so.

When Travis finally got the stick, the Kane anchorman was more than fifty yards ahead of him. Travis made a race of it, probably the most exciting of the day, but it was in vain. We lost. We lost the relay and the meet by one point.

There was no doubt about it. It was my fault. I was miserable. The guys tried to make me feel better, but it was no use. I knew it wasn't life or death, but we had wanted to beat them so badly. Even with Travis's four firsts, we had lost. How could we be expected to win the state meet?

Travis talked with me at my house that evening. "You know what we ought to do, Dal. We ought to switch positions. That way, if they put their fastest guy up first, I'll whip him and demoralize them. And if they don't, I'll give us a lead that no one can lose. Not even you."

He was smiling, and he punched me on the shoulder. I laughed. "Not even me, huh?"

"Not even you. I'm not braggin'. I just think it will work."

"I know. And you're right. Let's do it."

11
The Big One

The day of the state meet dawned bright and crisp. We couldn't have been more excited if Christmas had come in the middle of the year. Travis Bourne showed up at my house a couple of hours before we were scheduled to leave for the meet, showing me how we would win seven of the twelve events and walk away with the biggest team victory in state history.

I liked his enthusiasm, but I frankly couldn't believe it. He had us down for two field event gold medals, but he wouldn't say which ones. Then he had pegged us to win all his specialties, reminding me again that he was not bragging. I assured him I knew that and understood and had no doubt that we would win the hundred, the two-twenty, the four-forty, and the long jump because of him.

"Bugsy may beat me in the long jump, Dallas, and I have to tell you, nothing would make me happier. He's really been coming along. Then, I think we can win the mile relay too."

"You really do?"

"Absolutely."

"But Kane County whipped us, and they have the best time in the state this year."

"Our new strategy will pull that off, Dal. I'll be so happy by that time, having won at three gold medals, that I'll give us the start we need, and you'll hang on to win it."

"But what if you get upset in one or two of your events? Or all three? Then you won't be happy."

"Then I'll just be that much more determined to make the mile relay the race of the day."

Travis was surprised when Jimmy and Cory appeared on the horizon, riding their bikes toward my place. "Wonder what they are doing here."

"Don't you know? Sure you do. We've talked about it. They come every morning, and we spend time together."

"Oh, you mean reading the Bible and all that?"

I nodded.

"I knew you did that, but I guess I thought you only did it on school days or something. You even do it on days of big meets and stuff?"

"It's even more important then. We pray for everybody's safety. We even do it on Christmas and other holidays. We decided that we can always do it when the three of us are home, no matter what's going on the rest of the day. You wanna join us?"

"Nah. I'll sit in the next room and listen."

Which he did. Afterward, he was pretty quiet, only not like he had been before when he was upset and sullen. Now he just seemed thoughtful.

He pulled me aside later. "You know, I think I might like to join you guys sometime soon, if it's all right. Just to see if I like it. OK?"

I nodded, trying to hide how excited I was and how badly I wanted to shout the news to the other guys.

On the way to the meet, Travis explained to all of us that even if our team won only three events, we would likely win the state championship. Toby was doubtful. "How can that be? We, or I should say you, won four firsts against Kane County, and we still lost that meet. And they'll be our toughest competition today, too."

"That's true, Toby, but they beat us with so many strong seconds and thirds because we had so few guys entered in each event. And, of course, anything we didn't win, they won. In this meet, we still plan to get a lot of firsts, but events we don't win will likely be won by one of the many other super teams in the meet, and the seconds and thirds behind us will be shared by a lot of others besides Kane County too."

By the time we got to the stadium, everyone was convinced, and we couldn't wait to get started. With all the teams entered, the first five places in each event won points. First was worth ten, second seven, third five, fourth three, and fifth one.

The first surprise of the day, to everyone except Travis, was that Jack won the shot put! He was so excited! He didn't quite understand it all, but Travis explained that the extra rest we gave him really paid off. He threw the shot nearly fifty-three feet, and he cried when he received his blue ribbon.

Travis had his arm around big retarded Jack as they headed for the javelin competition. As they passed me I heard Travis talking to him. "You know, Jack, you're even stronger with the javelin. Use your excitement and your strength, and you can get another medal. You want one, don't you?"

"I sure do." Jack looked determined. On his first two throws, he was so eager that he fouled on one and threw poorly on the other. As he sat waiting for his final toss, Travis coached him. "Even your normal throw should get you about a third place, Jack. Just take it easy and throw the best you can, and you'll get us some points."

Jack threw his best ever and took another first. We thought he was going to float home! The way Travis had it figured, all we had to do was place in a couple of other events, and we would win the meet.

But the guys were so enthusiastic over our dominating the first two events, they wanted it all. They wanted the biggest state victory ever. When Toby got a completely unexpected fifth place in the discus, we found ourselves with twenty-one team points already. Teams had won the state meet with fewer points than that before.

Jimmy was a little disappointed to have finished sixth in the discus, just one place away from scoring, but he never let anything get him down for long and became a cheerleader for everyone else.

Cory finished seventh in the high jump but was pleased with his best jump ever. The surprise of surprises came in the long jump where neither Travis nor Bugsy took a first place. A little guy from way down state beat them both by four inches. Bugsy had the jump of his life to edge Travis by an inch, and the second and third for the Baker Street Sports Club gave us twelve points in the event and thirty-one team points!

Of course, we didn't have anyone entered in the pole vault, but the winners didn't bring their teams much closer to us.

In the one-hundred-yard dash, Travis won going away, and I finished fifth, so we got another eleven points for forty-two. In the two-twenty, Travis was first, Brent was fifth, and I was sixth (just out of the running for points). But that gave us another eleven for fifty-two.

It was clear now that no one could catch us. Even if we had pulled our entries from all the rest of the races, the only way anyone could even come close was if one team took first and second place sweeps of all the rest of the events.

Travis finished first and Bugsy fourth in the quarter mile to give us thirteen more points—sixty-two. That was when one of the officials approached me with some news.

"You know, son, the highest point total by any state championship team in history was seventy back in nineteen forty-six. You've got a chance to break that if you can score well in the last three events."

I gathered the team around and told them the news. Just while I was saying it, it was also being announced over the loud speakers, and the crowd was cheering us. The announcer was also telling everyone about our club and how we were self-coached and all that.

Bugsy shook his head. "Nineteen forty-six? That was before my dad was born!"

We all laughed and decided to cheer on Bugsy in the half mile and Ryan in the mile. We yelled ourselves hoarse. Bugsy started so fast in the half that he was leading by ten yards with a lap to go, but then he ran out of gas. In the final turn he was passed by one, then another, and another, and finally another.

His fifth place picked us up just one point for sixty-three, and he sat sobbing in the grass.

Travis spoke to him. "Get your strength back, and you can make up for it in the mile relay."

I reminded Ryan that with Travis and Bugsy in the mile relay, all he had to worry about was the mile, but he had one of the worst races of the year. He had been one of our hopefuls for a second or a third, but he finished dead last.

Only after the race did we discover that he had been running on a sprained ankle he had told no one about. We thanked him for trying so hard and told him not to feel too bad about it.

An hour later, as we loosened up for the mile relay, we knew what the situation was. A second place wouldn't do it. That would give us just seven points and would only tie us with the record. Only a first would break it by giving us seventy-three.

Kane looked to be our only competition in the mile relay, and they were eager to keep us from the record. We had their best athlete from the previous year, and they were a distant second in this meet with fewer than forty points. The best they could do in this event was to set a new state record, win the gold medal, and keep us from the team point record.

We had decided to run Travis first, then Brent, then Bugsy, then me, no matter how Kane lined up its team. I was sure they'd go with the same lineup that beat us before, but maybe they guessed that we were going to make a switch.

When the race began, their best man was set to run the anchor leg against me. I was scared to death. But Travis's strategy was perfect. He blew into the lead from the gun and was so far ahead by the halfway point that he demoralized the rest of the competitors.

Kane was the only team even close as he came around the far turn and handed off to Brent. Brent maintained the thirty-five yard lead most of the way and handed off to Bugsy, who had something to prove.

He was running against one of their strongest quarter milers, one who had finished ahead of him in the open quarter mile, so he wanted to keep the lead. The other man kept creeping up on him, but Bugsy fought him off, giving me a ten-yard lead on the second best quarter miler in the state.

I took off like a scared jackrabbit. I didn't feel comfortable. It was as if I was trying to run faster than I was really able. But I was flying, and I knew it. Usually I couldn't hear the roar of the crowd or my teammates, but this time I heard every word. Second place wouldn't do it! We wanted the record.

Somehow I had actually lengthened the lead over the first three hundred yards, but now I was paying for it. The legs, the arms, the body were gone. My breath came in huge gasps as I tried to hang on.

Coming around the second to last curve I saw the scoreboard with the standings and the scores staring me in the face. Around the last curve I could hear the Kane anchorman gaining on me. It was as if he was reeling me in. I had to hold on.

Into the final straightaway he was right on my heels and gaining. I fought and fought to hold him off. The finish line was a blur that seemed to be getting farther away, not closer. I felt lightheaded, almost dizzy, and my arms were leaden like my legs.

I could feel his footsteps pounding the asphalt right behind mine. Then he moved to my right to pass. If there was anything left in me, I reached for it. For the last twenty yards we ran neck and neck, then we both dove across the line, rolling and sliding and scraping our bodies.

It took the officials almost five minutes to study the video tape of the finish and decide.

We had won! The record was ours.

Moody Press, a ministry of the Moody Bible Institute, is designed for education, evangelization, and edification. If we may assist you in knowing more about Christ and the Christian life, please write us without obligation: Moody Press, c/o MLM, Chicago, Illinois 60610.